anythink

BRIGHT!
LIGHT ENERGY

Emma Carlson Berne

PowerKiDS press™

New York

Published in 2013 by The Rosen Publishing Group, Inc.
29 East 21st Street, New York, NY 10010

First Edition

Editor: Jennifer Way
Book Design: Andrew Povolny

Photo Credits: Cover Adam Kazmierski/Vetta/Getty Images; pp. 4, 10, 12, 15, 17 (bottom), 21 iStockphoto/Thinkstock; p. 5 Medioimages/Photodisc/Thinkstock; p. 6 Comstock/Thinkstock; p. 7 Superstock/Getty Images; p. 8 Sally Anscombe/Flickr Select/Getty Images; p. 9 Steve Cole/Digital Vision/Getty Images; p. 13 (left) Malcolm MacGregor/Flickr/Getty Images; p. 13 (right) Rob Marmion/Shutterstock.com; p. 14 Kidstock/Blend Images/Getty Images; p. 16 Karl Weatherly/The Image Bank/Getty Images; pp. 17 (top), 22 Hemera/Thinkstock; pp. 18–19 Jamie Grill/The Image Bank/Getty Images; p. 20 F1online/Thinkstock.

Library of Congress Cataloging-in-Publication Data

Berne, Emma Carlson.
  Bright! : light energy / by Emma Carlson Berne. — 1st ed.
      p. cm. — (Energy everywhere)
  Includes index.
  ISBN 978-1-4488-9649-3 (library binding) — ISBN 978-1-4488-9756-8 (pbk.) —
  ISBN 978-1-4488-9757-5 (6-pack)
  1. Light—Juvenile literature. I. Title.
  QC360.B476 2013
  535—dc23

2012020045

Manufactured in the United States of America

CPSIA Compliance Information: Batch #W13PK4: For Further Information contact Rosen Publishing, New York, New York at 1-800-237-9932

CONTENTS

WHAT IS LIGHT ENERGY?

Any time you flip on an electric switch or get up out of a chair, you are using energy. Energy is the ability of a system to do work. Energy comes in many different forms. Sound and heat are types of energy. Light is energy, too.

You use light energy every evening when you turn on the lights in your home.

One example of this kind of energy is the powerful rays of light energy and **radiant** energy that the Sun sends beaming toward Earth. Without this giant ball of light energy, life on Earth would not be possible. This book will explore all types of light energy. It will explain how we see light and how light is measured.

The Sun is likely the first source of light energy you think of. This book will show you other sources of light energy and explain the things this form of energy does.

A BRIGHT WORLD

Our world is filled with different sources of light. Think of the Sun's hot rays shining on your face. Picture a lightbulb glowing into brightness when you flick the switch. Think of the rosy glow of a campfire or lightning flashing during a storm.

Everything we see is light. We think we are seeing objects. What we are really seeing is the light that is **reflected**, or bounced, off of those objects. If you were to look at your cat, for instance, you are not seeing the cat. Instead, you are actually seeing only the light reflected off the cat.

Light reflects differently off of this cat than off of other objects. These differing light reflections affect how we see and recognize objects around us.

Thomas Edison

THOMAS EDISON'S LIGHTBULB

Thomas Edison was an inventor who lived from 1847 until 1931. He designed the first long-lasting incandescent lightbulb in 1879. This type of lightbulb is still widely used today.

7

WHAT ARE LIGHT WAVES?

Light energy travels in waves. If you were to watch the ocean waves roll toward the shore, you would be seeing a good example of how light waves travel. When light energy is **emitted**, or let out from a source, it travels in waves.

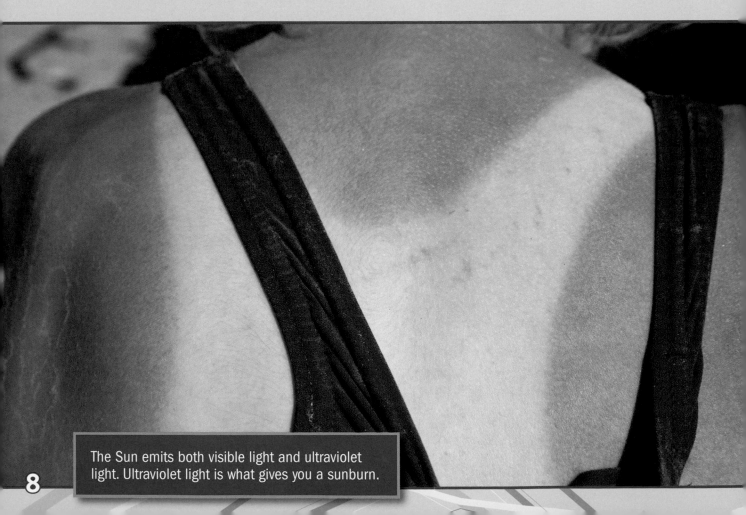

The Sun emits both visible light and ultraviolet light. Ultraviolet light is what gives you a sunburn.

If you could see these light waves, you would notice they have peaks and valleys like ocean waves. The peaks and valleys have different wavelengths, or distances between the peaks and valleys, depending on the type of light. For instance, the light you can see, **visible light**, has peaks and valleys that are farther apart than those of **ultraviolet** light.

VISIBLE AND INVISIBLE LIGHT

When you say "light," most people think of the light you can see. This visible light is actually only a small portion of all the light that exists. Light exists on the **electromagnetic spectrum**, which is a band of all the different kinds of light and radiant energy that exist. The light on the spectrum moves from longer wavelengths to shorter wavelengths.

This image was made using a camera that picks up the infrared energy given off by the body heat coming from a person's hand.

THE ELECTROMAGNETIC SPECTRUM

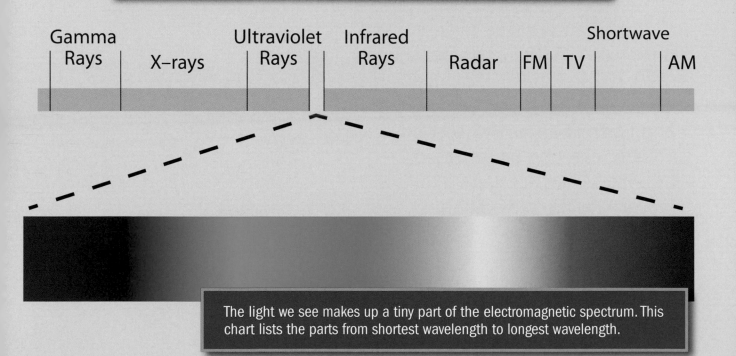

| Gamma Rays | X–rays | Ultraviolet Rays | Infrared Rays | | Radar | FM | TV | Shortwave | AM |

The light we see makes up a tiny part of the electromagnetic spectrum. This chart lists the parts from shortest wavelength to longest wavelength.

The Sun, for instance, emits several different kinds of light on the spectrum. It emits **infrared** light, visible light, and ultraviolet light. Each of these different kinds of light exists in a different place on the spectrum.

THE SPEED OF LIGHT

Light travels at the fastest speed in the universe, 186,282 miles per second (299,792,458 m/s)! This means that light can travel between the Moon and Earth in about 1.3 seconds!

Light can also be reflected, or bent. When you look in a mirror, you are seeing light reflecting. A rainbow is an example of a light wave breaking apart and showing the colors that make up a wave of visible light. The colors will always be in the same order. That order is red, orange, yellow, green, blue, and violet.

The distance between Earth and the Moon is about 238,900 miles (384,500 km).

You sometimes see a rainbow when the Sun comes out while it is raining. This is because the Sun's light is being bent by the raindrops in the air.

You use a mirror's reflection to make sure you do not have toothpaste on your face. Your parents use mirrors while driving to see what is behind them without having to turn around.

OUR AMAZING EYES

When light hits our eyes, the eye focuses by tightening or relaxing the muscles within the eye to control the amount of light that is let in. The light bouncing off of what you are looking at is then projected into the eye and onto the **retina**. Cone-shaped cells on the retina help us see visible light and colors.

Your pupils are the dark spots in the middles of your eyes. They expand to let in more light or contract to let in less light.

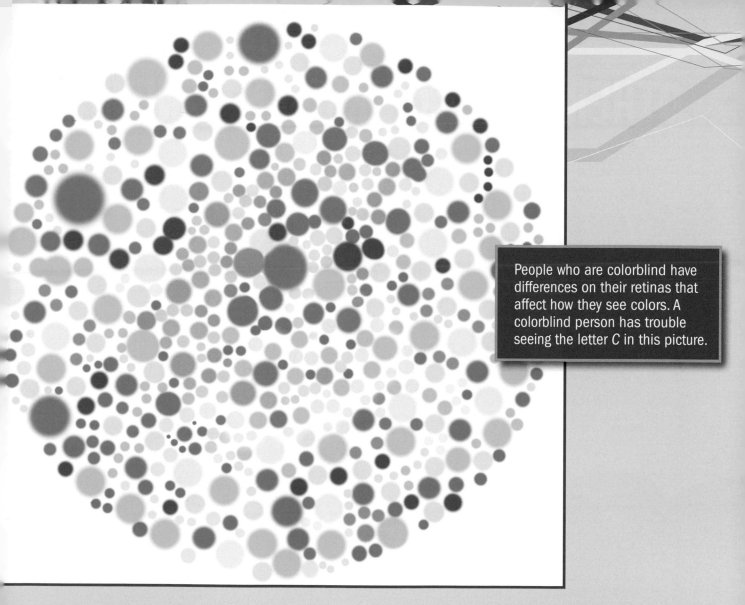

People who are colorblind have differences on their retinas that affect how they see colors. A colorblind person has trouble seeing the letter *C* in this picture.

The eye then converts the image on the retina into millions of electrical signals. Then the signals are sent through the **optic nerve** to the brain. When the brain receives these signals, it interprets them as the image we see.

OTHER KINDS OF RADIANT ENERGY

In addition to the visible light we can see, there are all sorts of light we cannot see. For example, infrared light is a type of **thermal** radiant energy. The heat from a campfire gives off infrared light and visible light.

Ultraviolet light is another example of light energy we cannot see. Ultraviolet light is in the Sun's rays as well as the special black lights you see that make things glow in the dark. If you had a broken bone, the doctor would probably order an **X-ray**. X-rays are another kind of light we cannot see.

A campfire gives off infrared energy, visible light energy, and heat energy. It can be used for light, cooking, and warmth.

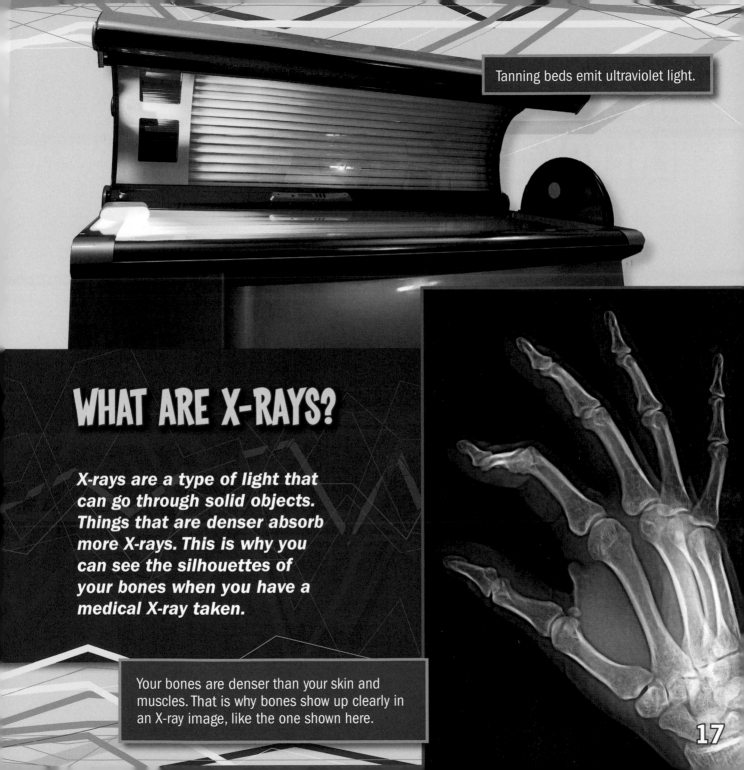

Tanning beds emit ultraviolet light.

WHAT ARE X-RAYS?

X-rays are a type of light that can go through solid objects. Things that are denser absorb more X-rays. This is why you can see the silhouettes of your bones when you have a medical X-ray taken.

Your bones are denser than your skin and muscles. That is why bones show up clearly in an X-ray image, like the one shown here.

17

HOW IS LIGHT ENERGY MEASURED?

There are several ways that light energy is measured. A unit called a candela tells how bright light is. One candela is about the amount of light given off by one candle. Visible light is often measured in a unit called a lumen, which tells how much light is coming from an object. One lumen is the amount of energy used to send one candela of light in all directions.

A light meter is an instrument used to measure light. It tells you how much light is in a certain area. Photographers use light meters, and many cameras have light meters in them.

This photographer is using a light meter near the woman being photographed. The light meter's measurement helps the photographer figure out the right setting for the camera.

CONVERTING LIGHT ENERGY

Energy is always changing into other forms. One of the most important rules of energy is that it cannot be created or destroyed. All energy is just being converted from one form to another.

Light energy can be converted into other kinds of energy. For example, a flower absorbs, or takes in, light energy from the Sun. It

Without the Sun's light energy, plants are unable to make their own food. They will then die.

Animals that eat plants do not directly use the Sun's light energy. They use it indirectly when they eat plants, though.

converts the energy into food for itself. Then a rabbit comes along and eats the plant. Now the energy stored in the plant will be converted into chemical energy in the form of food that fuels the rabbit's body.

EFFICIENT ENERGY

When energy is converted, some of it is converted into a form we can use. The rest, though, escapes into forms that go unused. For example, an **incandescent lightbulb** gives off light as well as heat. The unused heat energy is thought of as wasted energy.

There are other kinds of lightbulbs that give off less heat. Because less heat energy is wasted, they are a more energy-**efficient** source of light.

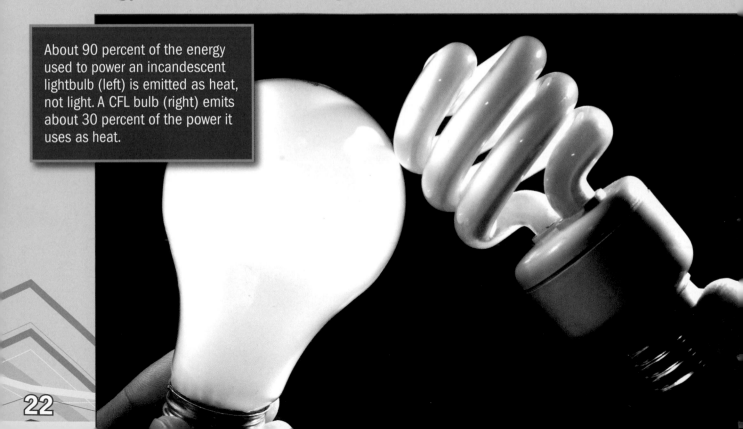

About 90 percent of the energy used to power an incandescent lightbulb (left) is emitted as heat, not light. A CFL bulb (right) emits about 30 percent of the power it uses as heat.

GLOSSARY

efficient (ih-FIH-shent) Done in the best way possible with the least waste.

electromagnetic spectrum (ih-lek-troh-mag-NEH-tik SPEK-trum) All the frequencies in which light waves, radio waves, and other waves can be found.

emitted (ee-MIT-ed) Put something into the air.

incandescent lightbulb (in-kun-DEH-sent LYT-bulb) An object that produces light when a piece inside the bulb is heated by an electric current.

infrared (in-fruh-RED) Light waves that are outside of the part of the light range at the red end, which we can see.

optic nerve (OP-tik NURV) The small tube that carries messages from the eye to the brain.

radiant (RAY-dee-unt) Giving off waves of light.

reflected (rih-FLEKT-ed) Threw back light, heat, or sound.

retina (RET-in-ah) The innermost layer of the eye that is very sensitive to light. It is connected to the brain by the optic nerve.

thermal (THER-mul) Using heat.

ultraviolet (ul-truh-VY-uh-let) Describing light that is off the visible spectrum at the violet end.

visible light (VIH-zih-bul LYT) Light that can be seen.

X-ray (EKS-ray) A special picture that can be taken of the inside of the body.

INDEX

WEBSITES

Due to the changing nature of Internet links, PowerKids Press has developed an online list of websites related to the subject of this book. This site is updated regularly. Please use this link to access the list: www.powerkidslinks.com/enev/bright/